W9-CRG-790

© 1993 Geddes & Grosset Ltd
Reprinted 1994
Published by Geddes & Grosset Ltd,
New Lanark, Scotland.

ISBN 1 85534 575 7

Printed and bound in Slovenia.

Rumpelstiltskin

Retold by Judy Hamilton
Illustrated by Lindsay Duff

Tarantula Books

Once upon a time in a small market town there lived a miller and his daughter. The miller was not a rich man, nor a famous or important man, but oh, how he wished he was!

He often lied to make himself sound important.

"My mill grinds faster than any other mill in the country!" he would claim. "Bread made with my flour rises twice as high as bread made with any other flour!"

But people paid little attention.

Then one day the king came to visit the town and the miller went too far.

"I have a daughter who can spin straw into gold!" he cried at the top of his voice.

Everybody gasped at this outrageous lie.

However, the king, who did not know of the miller's boasting, thought that he was telling the truth.

And the king was a greedy man!

He ordered that the miller's daughter be brought to the palace at once. When she arrived, he took her to a room which he had filled with straw, and had a spinning wheel brought to her.

"Spin this straw into gold before tomorrow morning, or you will die!" he commanded, then left the room and locked the door.

The poor girl could do nothing but cry. She could not spin straw into gold of course, and now, because of her father's foolishness, she would die

Suddenly a strange little man appeared.

"What's the matter?" he asked.

The miller's daughter told him everything.

"Perhaps I could help," said the little man.

"What will you give me in payment?"

"Take this," said the girl and handed the little man her necklace.

Without another word, he sat down at the spinning wheel.

'WHIRR - WHIRR - WHIRR.'

The girl watched in amazement as reel upon reel was filled with golden thread. As the little man worked, she fell asleep.

When she awoke the next morning, the man had gone, and the room was full of gold.

The princess could not believe her luck. The little man had saved her life.

When the king came into the room he was delighted. This girl must have magic powers!

However, he was a greedy man, and one roomful of gold somehow just didn't seem enough.

He wanted more!

"Well done, my child. You may live. But I cannot let you go, for I have more work for you," he said.

The king took the miller's daughter to a bigger room this time, crammed full of straw.

"Unless you spin all the straw in this room into gold by morning, you will die!" he said once more, and locked her in for another night.

The poor girl was in despair. Once again, she sat down on a heap of straw and wept as if her heart would break.

But she need not have worried, for all of a sudden the same little man who had helped her the night before appeared in front of her.

"I can guess what you want, but what will you give me in payment this time?" he asked.

The miller's daughter dried her tears and handed the little man her tiny silver ring.

Once again the little man sat down and began to spin.

'WHIRR - WHIRR - WHIRR.'

The miller's daughter fell asleep and next morning awoke once again alone in a room full of gold.

The king was truly amazed when he came into the room a little while later.

"A girl who can spin straw into gold would make me a fine wife," he thought to himself.

He took the girl to an even bigger room, once more filled with great bundles of straw.

"I like you," he said to the girl. "Spin this straw into gold before tomorrow morning, and I will marry you and make you my queen."

He led the girl into the middle of the room and then turned and left, locking the door behind him.

The king had hardly left the room when the little man appeared again.

"More straw then ever, I see," he said. "How will you pay me to change this lot into gold?"

The miller's daughter looked terribly worried.

"I have nothing left to give you," she said.

"Then you must make me a promise," said the little man.

"Anything—I will promise you anything!" cried the girl. The little man smiled at her.

"You must promise me that when you marry the king I can have your first-born child," he said.

It was a terrible thing to ask of her, but the miller's daughter had no choice but to agree. Besides, it would be a long time before she had a child. Perhaps the little man would forget her promise.

Once more, the little man set to work.

The king was overjoyed when he saw all the gold the next morning. He need never ask the girl to spin for him again, for he now had more gold than he would ever be able to use. He told the girl this, and asked her to be his queen. She agreed.

In time the miller's daughter came to love the king, and a year after they were married, they had a beautiful baby.

The queen was so happy in her new life that she forgot her promise to the strange little man.

But he had not forgotten. One day as the queen played with her baby in the nursery, he appeared again.

"I have come to take the child that you promised to me," he told her.

The queen was desperate, and clutching her baby close to her, she pleaded with the little man.

"You can have all my riches," she said, "but please, please leave my baby!"

The little man saw her distress and felt sorry for her, so he decided to give her one chance to keep her baby.

"I tell you what," he said, "I have a very unusual name." The girl looked puzzled, but the little man went on.

"If you can find out what my name is within the next three days, you can keep your baby."

With that, the little man left once more.

The queen frantically called her courtiers and enlisted their help, thinking of all the names that they could.

After a sleepless night, the queen sent messengers out all over the country in search of unusual names. When the little man came that day, the queen had a long list of strange names to read to him. But as she read each one, the odd little man shook his head, smiling. The queen was upset, and the next day had an even longer list to read to the little man. But still he only shook his head.

The queen was terribly afraid of losing her baby.

Then one of her messengers returned to the palace.

"Your majesty," he said, "I was coming back through the great forest when I came to a small clearing. There I saw the strangest little man dancing round a fire, and this is what he was singing,"

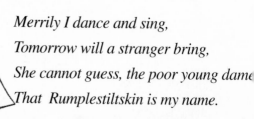

Merrily I dance and sing,
Tomorrow will a stranger bring,
She cannot guess, the poor young dame
That Rumplestiltskin is my name.

"That's him!" cried the delighted queen. All fear gone, she sat down to wait.

When he arrived, she was very calm.

"Is you name Balthazar?" the queen asked.

"No!" The little man shook his head.

"Is you name Ezekiel?"

"No!"

"Is your name, by any chance, Rumpelstiltskin?"

The little man was absolutely furious. "The fairies must have told you!" he screamed, jumping up and down in his rage.

Still yelling, the little man ran from the palace, leaving the queen and her baby safe together.

That was the last the queen ever saw of the little man called Rumpelstiltskin.

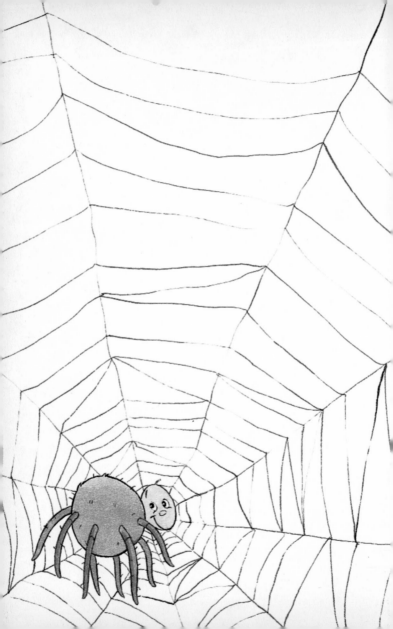